Kitty Shows Kindness

written by Dr. Mary Manz Simon
illustrated by Linda Clearwater

© 2003 Mary Manz Simon. © 2003 Standard Publishing, Cincinnati, Ohio. A division of Standex International Corporation. All rights reserved. Sprout logo is a trademark of Standard Publishing. First Virtues™ is a trademark of Standard Publishing. Printed in China. Project editor: Jennifer Holder. Design: Robert Glover and Suzanne Jacobson. Scripture taken from the HOLY BIBLE, NEW INTERNATIONAL VERSION®. NIV®. Copyright © 1973,1978,1984 by the International Bible Society. Used by permission of Zondervan. All rights reserved. ISBN 0-7847-1408-8

09 08 07 06 05 04   9 8 7 6 5 4 3 2

Standard
PUBLISHING
CINCINNATI, OHIO

www.standardpub.com

Kitty, Kitty, share today, what the Bible has to say...

Kindness means
I am aware
when someone needs
help and care.

If I see
someone in need,
that's when I do
a kind deed.

When the sun
is burning hot,
I show friends
a shady spot.

When someone
is scared at night,
I purr,
"Everything's all right."

If I'm tempted
to be cruel,
I recall
the Golden Rule.

People may be
kind to you,
if you're kind
and loving, too.

God is very kind to me.
He cares for me tenderly.

God shows me
what I should do.
Do you show
such kindness too?

"Be kind to everyone."
2 Timothy 2:24